LIFE HAPPENED

LIFE HAPPENED

IN BETWEEN THE PAGES OF MY DIARY

BIKKY KUMAR RAI

In memory of my father, Hriday Shanker Rai, and with love to my mother, Kanti Devi, and brother, Bikash Rai.

Prologue

It has been 3 long years since we both lost her, and today is her death anniversary.

I have been doing preparations for the puja from morning and he was looking for all the arrangements.

"Pragati, Panditji has arrived and is calling for you," Dadi called me.

"Coming down ",I replied.

I went down and gave Panditji all the items and he started the preparations.

"Pragati, bring out the clothes of Vibhor, it is in the closet in his room," Dadi said.

I went to my dad's room and started searching the clothes in the closet, then a mouse just passed me in a turbo speed, which brought a yeep from my mouth and startled me a bit, which knocked down a box from the top shelve.

"Ohh man, now I need to arrange these all," I groaned.

The things of the box were out open, I started packing the things up, but one thing caught my attention. It was an old diary.

"Never seen before this, it looked old," I thought.

It was an old diary most probably 10 years old, a bit rough on the edges, papers sticking out from it.

"Maybe belonged to mother," I thought.

As we all know curiosity killed the cat, so I decided to sneak-peek into it and guess what, I was totally wrong.

It belonged to my Dad, never imagined him as a guy who used to write ,let alone maintain one diary.

The first thing I saw was a picture of my Dad along with his school buddies from his teenage days.

“He has not changed a bit, same old face just aged a bit, and the paunch just got bigger,” I chuckled.

I thought to keep that diary for myself to read it later, I kept it aside and packed the other things in the box and bring out the clothes from the closet for him.

When I was coming out of the room, I saw the picture of the most beautiful woman; I kissed it and moved out from the room.

“Dad, your clothes are out on the bed, go quickly and change and come for the puja, Panditji is calling,” I said.

After some time, the puja started and ended late in the evening ,it was a hectic day, and the night called in for.

I was resting and thought about that time when I was angry with him, He loved her so much but did not even shed a tear when she died. I had stopped talking to him for months, he would wake me up and make me get ready for school, but I did not respond to him.

Things got better when I realized my mistake. One fortunate night when my sleep abruptly broke ,I came down to drink water ,I saw him on the swing with her photo in his hand and he was crying, he was crying ,when she died, he didn’t shed a tear and now I saw him crying with her photo in his hand

“I must be hallucinating, or it’s just a dream,” I thought.

I cannot get the things out of my mind, I decided to watch for few days and then confront him, so for the next few days I watched as the events unfolded Infront of me, the same sequence would repeat repeatedly.

When I decided to ask him about the things, my Dadi stopped me and revealed everything to me that since she had died ,there's not even a single day has passed he had not cried for her, he tried to remain unaffected Infront of me but eventually broke down when the night falls. Every night he would take her photo or things which was close to her with him and would sit down on the floor and would cry his heart out and eventually will cry himself to sleep.

Dadi said that she has never found him on his bed after that ,he was found on the stairs or on the swing, on the floor but never on the bed. I realized my mistake but was too guilty to confront him now. I cried that night and decided it is time to make up to him for the things I did it to him.

The very next morning when he came to wake me up , "Good morning teetu, get ready for the school", he said.

Teetu was the nickname he has given to me, "I will not go to school today, Daddy, I am not feeling well," I winked .

Seeing my antiques he smiled at me and said "Ok ,If you don't want ,skip today."

He actually smiled ,I saw him smiling after a long time and he really looked cute while smiling.

After that things turned normal between us ,but still he was never found on his bed at night.

I was brought out of my flashback when the phone beeped, I saw the time ,it was extremely late, so I decided to rest for the night and view the new prized possession later on.

"Good morning Teetu, did you sleep well, yesterday was a hectic day," Dad asked?

"Good morning, Dad it was ok," I replied.

"Acha now get ready for the school, or you might get late, breakfast is ready ,come quickly," he said.

"Dad as I was saying, can I skip classes for like 10 days please", I insisted.

"Why," he raised his brow.

"I would like to stay at home doing nothing, please don't say no to these", I made a puppy face, and I knew he can never say no to my puppy face.

"Ok my drama queen you can take your vacations," he said and ruffled my hair.

"Thanks dad," I quickly hugged him.

After that we had our breakfast and Dadi went to temple and Dad to office, I went to my room and took out the diary and started reading it. The first thing I came across was a picture of group of friends together in their late teenage years.

. I flipped the picture, and it was written "2nd April 2014" on the back of the photo and there were some names, "To Vibhor, Venkat, Santanu, Suvon, Mikey, Mitesh, Prit" ."To the unbreakable bonds". They were all really looking incredibly happy.

"*Dear D, you know today a weird incident happened and it is still the embarrassing one of my life*."

"Who names his diary D and talks to it while writing well if he can name his daughter Teetu he can do that as well," I chuckled.

"As I ,Mitesh and Mikey went to give our entrance exam ,we went to a mall afterwards ,wait that is not embarrassing , it's going to come we went to the fbb section and bought some chips and cold drinks and went to the cafeteria section to eat those. A security guard came and advised us to leave that place as outside eatables were not allowed. We tried to reason with him that we have brought this things in the mall itself, but he didn't budge, so we had to leave. We were leaving but what came upon us we directly went to washroom and waited there ,we were to leave but we saw Avik and his friends entering so we hid inside the compartment to surprise them afterwards, but they were taking time, so we decided to eat the chips there only. We were inside there for more than 10 minutes ,suddenly we heard a knock ,first of all we avoided it ,but the knocks increased, Mitesh answered but then it was bangs and it ordered us to vacate it. When we came out, we saw a group of guards standing outside and we felt like a terrorist group surrounded by defence personnel. They questioned us that what we were doing together inside it, we answered all of them by saying that one of the guards did not allow us to eat in the cafeteria ,so we were eating there and actually we were not lying. They let us go but forbade us to trying this type of thing again in the future, we nodded and with our heads down we left the place. It was so embarrassing, and I am never going to that place D".

"Whaaat ,Did I read it right, aww yuck it was so gross, how can he eat in a toilet, I should not have read that, but it was way too funny for teenage boys", I laughed out.

"You know today was our entrance exam we went to our test centre, fortunately I ,Mitesh and Mohammad were in one room and Venkat and Pandey were in other. As you know my luck is the best thing when it comes to things like these, I was to seat first ,then a vacant seat and then Mitesh and then all other participants. I was not prepared so I decided to play pick the odd one out and like that I completed my exams in just 30 minutes, and I slept for the rest of the exams. Mitesh next in partner was from an Engineering college and Mohammad's lot was also good. When our exam ended Venkat explained his part of story ,Venkat and Pandey got the chance of sitting next to a girl and we all know girls are better at academics than boys ,so they have a better chance among us."

I had seen his friends, and they all have changed a bit from their old pic

Vibhor- My Dad ,by the looks in the pic he has not even changed a bit, same round face ,just he has gained more weight now.

Mitesh- I remember him Dad calls him as baba ,I don't know why, skinny guy with a spec on him, slightly religious . He stills has a spec and is no more the skinny one, now the average type uncles.

Mikey- School stud I think, earrings, fancy hairstyles and fancy jewellery he is wearing. Now no more fancy jewelleries and hairstyles gained some weight, maybe marriage has changed him.

Santanu-a typical bong guy, average height .More or less looks the same now

Prit-typical fair guy with freckles on the face, taller than everyone. Has not changed just the freckles are more now

Venkat- the tallest of all, South-Indian guy with specs. Not changed at all

Suvon- the bodybuilder types, not tall by any means but more than average height. Now is the fattest among all.

They all sometimes visit along with their wives, aunty Shreyasi wife of Mitesh uncle and aunty Nina wife of Uncle Mikey were school friends and married two best friends too. Aunty Alya wife of Uncle Venkat were friends with aunt Saumili. Aunty Saumili wife of Uncle Prit ,I found her cute ,they love me more and they always bring something for me whenever they come to visit us. Looks like friends married each other friends.

OH, what a crazy gang of friends, adulthood has changed them all. Dad used to do this kind of stuffs in his childhood day that is why he never stops me from doing any activities.

When Dad arrived from office, he took me for dinner to their favourite dining place where he and mom used to have dinner. After dinner ,he also treated me to an ice-cream . What a perfect way to spend an evening

With night drawn in ,I retired to sleep.

As I flipped through Dad's old diary, I stumbled upon a wild story about his school trip to Digha.

Finally, our vacation made it out of our WhatsApp group, although it is not that far from our homes, but a vacation is a vacation, nonetheless.

I chuckled at how excited Dad and his friends were!

Mitesh booked our bus tickets, and I planned our itinerary, but there is nothing to plan for itinerary, the main plan was booze and beach.

Typical schoolboys!

The destination is Bengal's favourite family picnic spot, Digha. We contacted with the bus driver and came to our boarding spot, as we were waiting for our bus to arrive, we took a selfie together and when the bus arrived, we boarded and took our seat.

After an hour or so , we reached our halt, Kolaghat. The chilly nights and the busy highways, and roadside dhaabas, all made our night. We ordered dim-toast and chaa, as it is known as egg-toast and tea.

I love how simple pleasures brought them joy!

We had our fill and quickly boarded again, and the journey resumed again. The bus reached its destination exactly at 04:30 am, and we had not booked our hotels yet, so we straightaway raced to the beachside and dipped our feet in the water, feeling its coldness.

We were in awe when we witnessed the sunrise, it was a lovely view, the scenic beauty can't be described in words, but the real fun started after that, as were awake the whole night, and the sun was up, we all got a severe headache, and the hotel check-in time was 09:00 am, and with each passing seconds, we were feeling it.

When the clocked ticked 9, we rushed to the nearest hotel and booked our rooms, completed the formalities, and entered our room, unloaded our luggage and as soon as we landed on the mattress, we felt a sigh of relief.

We napped the whole afternoon, and in the evening our real plan started. Santanu and Mikey went for booze shopping and Suvon, me and Mitesh went out to gather our dinner and chakna.

I can sense the excitement building up!

We bought 2 kgs of chicken and divided it equally, one kg as chicken curry and the rest as for pakodas. While we were gathering other supplies, Santanu bought India's favourite drink, the Old Monk and some cold drinks for a non-drinker like me.

Dad, the sober one!

Yup, I forgot to tell you, I was the non- drinker of our group, the saviour of the moment, the sober one. We gave the chicken in the restaurants hotel and placed our orders and went back to our room. Till the time, our order was getting ready, we plugged in some music to set the mood and were gossiping. When the staff came to deliver our order, he asked if we wanted anything else and he said " Deluxe lagbe", which initially we didn't understand, he was asking if we want any hookers, he can arrange that too, but we declined laughingly.

And then our party started, drinks were poured down and I kept a bottle of thums up for the feel. One peg down, next peg down, after 3-4 pegs the mahol was setting up as the daaru was kicking in. Mitesh gulped the neat pegs and the first one to get super-duper high, others were in control till now and were leg pulling him, which we definitely can't understand, given his current situation. Suvon and Mikey started teasing him, making him do some activities, for instance, Suvon asked him, how cash comes out of an atm, Mitesh responded to this " Paisa nikalta hai krrr krrr karke", and we all were laughing holding our stomach.

Then we volumed up the music and started dancing to Bhangra hits, old retro songs, party hits, they were drinking their share of rum, and I was drinking my share of cold drink. A bit of heated exchange happened between Mitesh and Santanu, as both were not in control and Mitesh said to Santanu, that we are drinking late because of you, and Santanu retaliated by saying, "if I am at fault, I am packing my things up and leaving for home right now, you all are not able to enjoy properly because of me, I will leave right now", and we just saw the scene and then glanced over the watch, it was 11:30 pm, Suvon rebuked him saying, "you wont get any bus now, leave tomorrow early morning", to which Santanu agreed to.

And in the split second, Santanu and Mitesh started dancing together. All were outside the room smoking and I was in the washroom, they didn't take the key, and I came out of the room without the key thus locking the door. Mikey said to me that we are drunk, yet you left the key inside, and all were laughing at my expense. Then we went to the reception and asked for a spare key, and they opened the lock for us. We ate our dinner and put the two overdosed drinkers to bed and bid goodnight to the night.

The next morning, both of them has no understanding of what happened the previous night. Today we planned for Udaypur beach, and we took a Toto and marched down to our destination. We booked a table and ordered some Amudi fries, some beers and sat nearby to the crashing waves.

Sounds like a perfect day!

The beer was costly there, still Santanu drank two beers, he was a beerholic, we ordered a chicken dish and some fruit-chaat. We sat there for a good one and a half hour, when we were leaving the beach, Santanu saw the shop owners taking beers from a place and he entered that place and asked the price there, it was cheap there as they have no sitting arrangement, Santanu bought a beer and drank it there itself, quoting "thoda sasta hain a waha se".

Dad's friends were something else!

Now the beer inside Santanu was talking, we were feeling sleepy, when we left the Toto at the stands, there was a beer shop, he went there and purchased a beer again, saying its cheap here, when we entered the room, the first one to pass out was him only. We all were tired, so we also slept through the afternoon, and Santanu was so drunk that his mobile received n number of calls from his dad, but he didn't pick up, when finally in the evening, he woke up from his deep sleep, horror ran through his face seeing the missed calls. He called back and his dad scolded him, and we were laughing in the corner. After the session his face was down, but on hearing about drinking again in the night, his face lit up and believe me that was not the brightest thing to do that night.

Mitesh again did the same thing, drinking only the neat pegs and going overboard.

I'm surprised they survived!

This time they were short on drink, so they asked the room service to deliver a bottle , when the room service came to deliver, we received and pranked Mitesh by saying to him that the room service is on call, please ask them to bring it inside, but on the other end was Mikey talking from the other room, he said to Mitesh " Sir, your bottle has been delivered, Love you", to which Mitesh said " kya mast room service hai , love you bolta hai".

As he was drinking, his actions became a little wild, he spanked Suvon and said, you got a great booty and then spanked again, Suvon was bewildered but he let it go in the fun. As the night deepened, his actions got more wilder, at last I hold him in a submission lock preventing all his extra moves draining his extra energy, but I too started laughing, when he started calling out, "Police – Police , bachao mujhe, koi mujhe pakad ke rakha hai". Eventually his energy died down, still we were in party mode, but our fun went down in the drain when Santanu and his loose stomach decided to let everything come up on the floor.

All the beers, spicy chicken, more rum, and food mixed up with the heavy movements created a river of puke when Santanu puked everything out and he fall asleep on the bed with all the puke out beneath him, he was comfortably sleeping with his mess around but it was too much for sober ones, me and Suvon unable to bear the smell opted to sleep outside in the hall on the couch.

In the morning, we called for room service to clean up the mess and we freshened up, check out and left for the bus. We took the hell's ride, SBSTC bus, which will drive like anything on the highways, not bothering for other vehicles or tight nook corners. When we left the bus and finally reached our destination, we felt relieved.

What an adventure! An adventure to remember!

Next morning Dad had an urgent meeting, so he had to leave early for the office. So, I continued my work of reading the secrets.

"D, today results were announced as I mentioned I had a little chance ,so we all met at our adda zone and discussed our results. I got 45 out of 150,Mitesh got 35 and he abused that engineering geek like anything, Mohammad got 30,amongst us Venkat and Pandey did the best ,they got 95 and 90 respectively but here lies the catch, when we breakdown their score they did well in the two subjects and got a negative one in the other, when we asked them about this mishap, they said due to some fault the girl was shifted to another system during the last phase of the exams ,so they have to guess and score the rest. We were laughing like anything D."

"Our college life starts now; we all are in different colleges across the state. I got my admission in Haldia Institute of Technology and is deep inside the countryside. Today is my first day of my college and I am very much nervous about it .Our orientation went well, and we were sent to our respective classes. I was feeling nervous, and I am missing those idiots now, but luckily, I made some friends Ravindra ,Bhubam, Shweta and Maryam. They are really nice people; let's see how it turns out."

"Today was an unfortunate day D, we had our first ragging ,some says ragging is an icebreaker ,some says it's a way to bring you out of your shell, I also believe the same but when done in limit, when done beyond that it's just pure abuse ,both physical and mental abuse. All the juniors were called to a

senior's room ,they ordered us to form a circle and sit and they surrounded us like pack of sheep are surrounded by lions to feast upon. One by one the introduction started, I was too nervous that I fumbled thrice and had to give intro like for 10 times.

It was going slight well till a drunkard senior came and slapped one of us twice. Though we wanted to say something, but it was like we choked on our own breath, some of the seniors seemed nice ,they took that drunkard away and dismissed us all, they also cannot do anything na, they cannot support juniors in front of their own kind. I had decided I will never take ragging of my juniors in my future.

I have witnessed some more events which can be termed funny excluding the physical abuse a couple of times. Once during the recess, I was returning back to my hostel, a senior caught up to me and he started asking normal questions as he recognized by my full formal attire, I had no other option but to answer him. As we reached his hostel, he asked me to accompany him, I refused initially but he insisted that it will be over in minutes, they just want to talk.

Once we were inside, he called out his friends and they started asking me intro questions to which I replied calmly though from inside I was too nervous, one of them was the Joint Secretary of College Committee, he asked me who among them looks rowdy,

I thought it to be a trap, so I replied to no one but they insisted and I replied the JS looks rowdy, then his friends told me that he is the class topper and joint secretary, but he jokingly said he will get it in written from me to present during his interviews, his friends were laughing, so do I . After the session they let me go as I was getting late for my classes.

One other incident was I was going to college in full formal attire except the shoes, I was wearing slippers with formal clothes, and I was entering the gate, a senior intercepted my way, he asked me to do one thing, either I should remove my slippers or I should remove my tie as it was a very awkward combination of tie with slippers, he asked me to quickly go and change my slippers. The other students were laughing in amusement."

Dad went through ragging and all, nowadays its non-existent in colleges, yes back then it was something different.

Let us dive in deep into the secrets.

"*Today was the first day after orientation, I cannot understand half of them what the professors are speaking. I choose a safe zone, the last of the row with Ravindra as my partner, Bhubam was two seats in front of me and to my diagonally end Maryam was sitting with Meetu, and Shweta with Aradhvi. Did not I told you about Meetu , I had not mentioned about anyone to you, D, ok let's start with them.*

Ravindra- he is from Bihar 5'4, a skinny lad and the best part he lacks the intellectuality that Biharis have, but he can very well do poetry.

Bhubam-Our Bong guy, from nearby area, 5'5, he is my teacher, he teaches me everything which I don't understand in class

Maryam-one of the cute girls of our class, she is of same height as me, she can tear our eardrums with her voice when angry, and the best features are her eyes and her caring attitude.

Shweta- She is a little chubby; she loves animals and loves eating rather than cooking food.

Aradhvi-She is the one Ravindra has fallen in love with on the first day, you know na love at first sight.

Meetu- The perfect bong beauty, she is 5'3 but looks perfect, her eyes describe the perfect bong naari, she had the perfect curly hair, and the best thing is her smile accompanied by her dimpled cheeks. Everything thing in her is perfect, else everything has flaws. I think I like her but will she also .I think I got the perfect reason to be present every day at college .When she speaks, it's like she is singing songs, so melodious, I wish I always listen to it, if I had a chance, I would never leave her from my sight."

Ohho Dad's got a crush during his college times, surely, he knows his way through words, now I know how he was able to woo mom, need to know more, I cannot contain my excitement now, I will complete this diary today only.

As I stepped into my college life, far away from home, I could not shake off the feeling of homesickness. Every little thing reminded me of my family and friends back home. The freedom that college offered was exhilarating, but it also made me feel lost and alone.

Dad, you were so homesick! I can understand why.

I would often find myself packing my bags and heading back home, extending my stay for weeks. My semester had started in early January, but I was too caught up in the comfort of my home to return sooner.

Finally, when I did return to college in late January, I was still adjusting. On my first day back, January 25th, I walked into my Engineering Drawing class feeling unwell. Professor Sharma noticed me slouching and asked if everything was alright.

"I'm finding it hard to cope with being away from home, sir," I said, feeling a lump form in my throat.

Professor Sharma nodded sympathetically. "It's normal, son. But you need to find a balance. Can't keep running back home every time you feel homesick."

You were really struggling, Dad. I'm glad Professor Sharma was understanding.

Little did I know, the conversation with Professor Sharma would be my only interaction with college life for a while. The very next day, January 26th, our college's cultural fest was set to begin, and I had zero interest in participating.

I packed my bags and headed back home, skipping college for another week. The fest would go on for seven days, and I saw no reason to stick around.

You missed the cultural fest? That sounds like so much fun! Why didn't you want to stay?

When I finally returned to college in mid-February, I was determined to catch up on missed classes. But my absence didn't go unnoticed.

The Head of Department (HOD), Professor Mukherjee, called me and my fellow absentees for a meeting.

As I entered his chamber, the warm sunlight streaming through the window highlighted the stern expression on his face. The bright day seemed to mock me, its radiance contrasting with the darkness of my situation.

"We've noticed your consistent absence, and it's affecting your academic performance," Professor Mukherjee said sternly. "You're all on thin ice. I want to speak with your parents."

Oh no, Dad! You were in trouble!

We exchanged nervous glances, trying to decline. "Sir, it's not necessary..."

But Professor Mukherjee was adamant. "I won't let you leave until I've spoken with them. Get their numbers."

We reluctantly provided the numbers, and Professor Mukherjee began dialing. However, fate had other plans.

The first call failed due to network connectivity issues. "No signal," his phone displayed.

Undeterred, Professor Mukherjee tried the next number, only to be met with a busy tone.

"All busy," he muttered, frustration creeping into his voice.

He tried repeatedly, but each call was met with a different obstacle: voicemail, out-of-service area, or simply no answer.

As the minutes ticked by, our anxiety grew. We knew our parents would be worried, but Professor Mukherjee's determination remained unwavering.

Finally, after what felt like an eternity, Professor Mukherjee slammed his phone on the desk.

"Fine," he said, exasperated. "I'll give you one last warning. Shape up or ship out."

Wow, Dad, that must have been scary!

As I exited his chamber, the once-bright day had transformed into a dark, foreboding evening. The sky seemed to darken with my mood, the shadows deepening as I walked away.

Days passed, and I continued to struggle with attending classes, especially Engineering Drawing. Attendance was marked based on drawings submitted to assistants, and I had missed several classes.

One day, I decided to turn things around. I sat diligently in class, drew meticulously, and when I showed my work to the assistants, they asked my roll number.

"FT-07," I replied confidently.

They checked their sheet, looked puzzled, and said, "But we've struck your name off. We thought you'd left college."

The class erupted in laughter, and I felt my face burn.

Oh, Dad, that must have been mortifying!

But I stood firm. "I've been attending classes, I swear."

The assistants looked sceptical but decided to cross-check with Professor Sharma.

"Sir, has this student ever attended your class?" they asked.

Professor Sharma smiled. "Actually, I had a conversation with him a few days ago. He's been struggling with homesickness."

The assistants checked my assignments, marked my attendance, and asked me to complete previous ones.

I felt relieved. " Thank you, Sir."

"Life at HIT is not so bad now, the early days were miserable as I missed home, those fucking idiots, food but now I have adapted myself. The classes are boring, the teachers' guardians of Hell, and the hostel food fucking worse than poison and I have my antidote with me which is Meetu.

The best thing about this place is its open space, it's cool breeze and the food served in the theks, the best being maggi bhaaza and hot ginger chai. You know today, Ravindra ,Bhubam and me travelled to Riverside ,its perfect for me, I think I am in love with this place D, its beauty ,the calmness, it soothes my mind, and the best part is the cool breeze flowing in relaxes you. After sitting there, we had our photographic sessions, and then we ate some street foods and then later returned to our hostel."

"Teetu can you please come down for a moment?" Dad called me.

"Coming Dad," I hid the diary and went downstairs.

When I went downstairs, I was surprised by the visit of his friends, Dad has asked them to come over for dinner, but little I knew that he has a surprise for me.

After dinner when I retired to my bed, when the clock hit 12 am ,I was surprised by the sudden loud sounds ,when I opened my eyes ,I saw everyone clapping and singing songs it was my birthday after all and I have forgotten but Dad didn't ,there was a cake.

“Happy Birthday Teetu,” Dad wished me.

“Happy Birthday Pragati,” Dadi and everyone wished me.

“Thank you all,” I replied with a smile.

After celebrations all went to sleep, Dad came up to me and asked, “missing mom, I know she was always the first to wish you first.”

I nodded with tears in my eyes, “I really do miss her dad, I really do.”

After dad left the room, I thought of the day when mom and dad first brought me home, I was brought up in an orphanage in Delhi but one day they came to that orphanage and luckily they selected me, after completing the process they brought me with them and since then they have ushered me with their love and never made me feel that I am their adopted daughter not their real one. Mom used to take me for shopping and then would call Dad to meet in a restaurant for lunch. Life was way so happy until one day she left us, she was ill from a few days but then suddenly we lost her.

The past memories lulled me to sleep. Though I remember any dream but this dream I didn’t want to forget ever. In my dream, I saw Ma and Dad holding my hands and we are walking down the lane, going to our favourite spot.

On my birthday, they would take me to the nearby mall and would buy me a present and then we always went out to eat. And this was the same mall, dad and his friends were caught, this information I got later on from his diary.

In my dream, I saw Ma buying me my favourite dresses and we are having a gala time, Dad as usual waiting outside and asking us to take whatever we want and not to spend any more seconds in there. We are laughing together; Ma is looking so pretty while laughing.

When we came out, Dad quickly snatched those dresses, went to the billing counter, and did all the formalities and we were travelling next to our favourite Biryani place. We ordered our usual order, Ma and Dad were feeding me with their own hands turn by turn, although, I can eat alone but I feel pampered when they did these lovable gestures. We all were having a fun time, but time does not stop by, right?

My alarm went off and I was awake, remembering those beautiful moments, I cried a bit, as I was not in a mood to wake up from the bed, I again, dozed off to sleep.

Today we fooled one of our professors, I know, it's not a good thing to do. Professor NC has given us an assignment many weeks before, and all the boys of the class forgot to that and we thought Sir has forgotten that, but today he asked us to bring that in our second half of the class.

The girls, as usual, has done their share of work, so we devised a plan, as we had little time left, we photocopied the assignment of Meetu, and thought of submitting it.

We cross- questioned ourselves that if Professor will examine it, so to cover our tracks, we attempted to make it look old, some of us crumpled their pages and some folded it and kept it inside the books and ruffed the edges, some even tore the sides, I just traced all of that with a black pen and then crumpled the page so that no one will understand that it's a photocopied paper and not a handwritten assignment. We were planning to minute details but somewhere in our mind, we knew that Professor will not even look at the assignment, so we submitted it.

One such instance where I was caught without doing anything, I should change my name to problem magnet because I attracts problems in my way wherever I go.

Our HOD has given us a project to do, this time I did my project on my own and completed it before time. My batchmates asked me to share it, so that they can complete theirs, I specifically told them to not to copy completely, only to take some points and rework it according to their project. All listened to my instructions, except one, he straightaway copied all of my project with each and every details including my name, he didn't even bother to change my name with his own, he submitted it as it is.

During our practical class, out of nowhere HOD called out my name, he asked me comically, why I have submitted my project twice and that too from other student's mail, till now I had no clue of what was going on, I was clueless and so do rest of the classmates.

All became clear when HOD talked all about the mishap, I couldn't help myself as everyone was laughing hearing this including HOD, he took it in a good sport and didn't scold us. He let us off the hook and asked the student to re-submit his assignment.

My project was evaluated irrespective of the incident that HOD found similarities in everyone's project as the base of all of them was almost the same, but mine was preferred first because I submitted it way before the rest of them, and the subject matter was very close to the project given.

Today was no different, like always Dad came to wake me up and he has his unique way of waking me up, he kisses me on my forehead and then wakes me up.

"Good morning Teetu and Happy birthday to you," he wished me smilingly.

"Thanks Dad, Dad please do not go to office today, we will spend some time alone together," I requested.

"Ok as my princess commands, it will be done," he said.

After we had our breakfast, I asked him about his college time without raising any suspicions.

"Dad how was your time in college, how was your friends, I met your school friends but know little about your college ones," I asked.

"My life in college was ok types, and I had few friends too mumma,moti,madhu,and rk",he responded.

I was taken aback by his statement, till now not heard a word about them in the diary, who were they? I thought.

"Who were they, not usual names right," I asked back.

"Ohh yes they were nicknames I used to call by them, Mumma was Maryam, Moti was Shweta, Madhu was Bhubam and Rk was Ravindra and then there was Meetu and your mom too," he replied childishly.

"What? Mom was from your college, and I did not know that "I facepalmed at his antics and his habit of nicknaming others.

"Yes, she was from a different department, and we met at the end of our 3rd year, I met her through Maryam in an event", he answered.

"Your mom and me had contacts with them when we were in Delhi, but after she died, I had no motive of staying there so I returned back to Kolkata with you, we all are busy in our lives, so we had little conversations now," he said.

"Tell me something more about them na," I asked.

"Not today, some other time," he said.

"Please dad, today is my birthday and you will decline me like this," I puppy faced and played my trick.

"Ok you won, and I lost," he started describing everyone.

After our breakfast was over ,he took me to a shopping spree and then bought me a gift, he made my day but that was not over yet, when we returned home ,a party was waiting for us ,he has planned that for me and in reality, I was surprised.

"It's been 2 years in college and my infatuations for Meetu has increased, the whole department knows this and maybe she also knew but I didn't had the courage to tell her, what if she is committed, what if she rejects ,we are now good friends and I don't want to lose her D. Mumma took me out and told me to take her out for a date or else she will tell her everything.

Initially I refused but later I gave in and with huge courage I asked her out. I was afraid but she accepted my invitation, and I was so relaxed. We went for an evening stroll twice in a week and this time I let her know my feelings and asked her out for a proper date, she nodded for a yes and I am on seventh cloud D,I cannot express how I am feeling.

The day arrived ,I was confused on what to wear ,I asked Ravindra to come and help me and I was panicking ,Ravindra was unable to control me and at last he called Maryam to calm me, Maryam scolded me hard and said its ok ,nothing to be panicked of, it will go well. So I went with a blue casual shirt and a denim below and casual sneakers, I waited for her outside the girls hostel Matangini as I wanted the maximum time to spend with her ,when she came out I was awestruck, she was looking gorgeous in her black top matching with her black jeans, I cannot describe in words D, I received her and gave her a chocolate and then we went for a stroll, when we were walking I cannot help myself from looking into her eyes, I wished the time to stop there only, and suddenly our hands touched each other and she hold my hands and in an instant I intertwined my fingers with hers and hold hers too, it was a magical feeling ,a feeling of pure bliss ,we walked for some time and then went to eat something. I was listening to her while she was explaining each and every thing in details, I forgot to tell na that she is such a chatterbox, she can speak throughout the day, and I can listen to her.

I did not want the evening to end, but it happened, and we came back. She returned to her hostel, and I waited until she went back, I can still feel the fragrance of her hands on my own and thus the date with beauty ended."

"D you won't believe what happened in class today, one of the Profs gave us a complex numerical to solve and you know I am a fucking Einstein at solving them so I decided not to, I was sitting next to Meetu ,she was solving it with great determination, she was chewing a gum and was looking adorable like that, I was playing with her free hand and she was asking to not to disturb her and let her concentrate but I didn't listen to her and placed a kiss on her hand. The whole class now knows about us ,so there is nothing to worry. She was chewing gum, solving it, and asking me to solve it too, but it was way above my level, if the topper is

having so much problem and then how come I can solve it, so I decided not to. She scolded me for being such reckless ,I just pouted and let my head down on the bench with my face towards her, she cannot resist my look and gave in ,she ruffled my hair ,winked, hold my hand, and placed a kiss on my hand. We went out of the class and went for the theks."

"He is such a drama queen, and he calls me one," I laughed inwardly.

"It has been months since we were together, she knows my feelings and I know hers, but never proposed her but I had thought I will propose her in our college cultural Techfest Riveira, I decided it to make a great experience for her , I had been preparing it for weeks now. All classes were suspended for the fest, and I was waiting for it.

On the evening of the first day I waited for her to come ,she wore a black gown and was looking ethereal ,she was dressed to kill that evening, we went to the event with me holding her hands ,I didn't want to leave her even for a second , the evening went well and I went to leave her till her hostel gate, while returning back she hugged me and placed a kiss on my cheeks, I kissed her on her forehead and hugged her tightly and returned back to my hostel.

I waited for the 2nd day to arrive so I can propose her, but today it was strange she was not receiving my calls nor texting back my messages. I called her roommate to make sure she was well, she said they are coming to the fest in a few minutes. When she arrived, she was acting weird, she had distanced herself from me and was just nodding. She excused herself and departed earlier that night and did not bother to text me back.

The very next day I called her many times; texted her but got no response. Then a message popped up she wanted to meet, I went to meet her but before I can ask anything she said that from now on she can't meet me, neither she will call me nor text me and I had to forgot her, I tried to reason with her but she won't listen ,she said it's for the betterment of both and left me alone in the road with my heart broken into thousand pieces and a deep pain residing inside. Even God knew this and to hide my tears ,say it incidentally or not it started to rain, I was just standing alone in the rain ,cannot understand what to do next, I was feeling like the purpose of my life was taken from me, I dragged myself to my room and cried that night."

"Wait, what just happened all of a sudden?" I thought.

"When a piece of glass breaks we can hear it breaking and see its pieces broken but when this tiny little heart breaks, it breaks into a thousand pieces, neither we can hear the sound nor we can see its broken pieces, we can only feel one thing, the pain the deep dying pain which doesn't leaves us even if we want to, and we can pacify ourselves and that pacification also doesn't helps."

"Well, that was deep," I pondered.

"I thought it to be a dream, but it was not, I went to college the next day in hopes of that everything will be fine but when I saw her, she straightaway ignored me like she has never seen me in the college.

That ignorance drove me to a point that I drank for the first time ,I tried each and every thing just to forget her as it was killing me ,my grades slipped away, I had retreated myself to a shell, I had lost connections with Ravindra ,Madhu, Mumma and Shweta .I had my first drink ,I had my first smoke and I had my first weed, I tried everything which will help me forget her".

"Well, I used to wonder why people smoke. I asked a few but their replies will not make any justifications like some would say it eases the mind, it relaxes you, and it has its own fun and so on. Different people different opinions, but I also made my mind to make my statement ,so one of my hostel mate offered his help to teach me this skill, he offered me a cigarette and asked me to take a puff inside and keep it inside my mouth for a few seconds and then leave the smoke through my nose. At first, I was hesitant to do so, but eventually gave in, I took my first puff ,at the first instant I choked on my own breath and coughed up a bit, he assured me that it happens for the first time and asked me to take another puff.

This time it was different, I felt relieved in that smoke, I enjoyed each and every puff and that was the start of a chain-smoker. Now my pocket always had a packet of cigarettes and events after events led to a different habit. It was a deep pit, I knew I was falling into it, but I cannot help myself, I was enjoying drowning into that pit.

As you know D, when you are into different not so good habits people tend to land you in other habits too, people call it experiences but they do not explain it to you whether it is good or not. So, I landed myself in becoming the ultimate bhakt of baba, in smoking weed or gaanja and its common in engineering colleges to get some although its illegal. Every hostel has a room which is the hub of weed smoking ,when you enter those, you will find yourself engrossed in smoke accompanied by dim light and soft music. I also reached one of such room in my hostel and the best part is that they don't treat anyone outsider, the sane minds differentiate peoples not the insane ones, when I reached inside I was given a seat and the chillum , the smoke was already pushing me into a different zone , I was unable to think clearly ,it was like I am flying ,I had no burdens. When I took a long puff from the chillum, I felt no difference but have you heard of the aftereffects, I was going to feel some right away, when I took more puffs, I was straightaway thrown in a state of trance, I had different emotions running throughout my mind , I was like whether I should cry or laugh ,should I live or die, whether I should sleep or be awake, should I run or crawl, I was hungry ,at the same time my stomach was full, I was tired yet energetic , I found myself yet still trying to find myself. I cannot make sense what I was going through. I found myself in seventh heaven, I smoked so much that I slept in that room for myself to awaken the next day."

"So many revelations in such few days, this is going to take a few more days to let that in, who would have thought that this cute looking father of mine has done such experiences" I let that in.

"*D this is something I had wrote after getting to know from others, I had my first drink, and I drank so much that I passed out and I do not remember a shit of what happened that night. I just remember what led to the events. For me life was still struggling to find its own path, but even an instance from past would leave it shattered to pieces again. As I was returning to my hostel I saw a familiar face, I saw Meetu with someone, at first I ignored it but what she did later just triggered my broken emotions, she fucking hugged that guy, yes you heard me right, she fucking hugged him and that hug was not any friendly hug, I left that place in a rage and that rage cost a window pane its life. My head was hurting, my heart was burning , I went to chillax hub as I have named it but to my dismay, they were not having baba today ,I was disappointed but later they told me they were going to drink, and I should join me.*

I accepted it and it's a common fact that everyone's first drink is never from their own wallet, they made a neat peg and asked me how much to dilute it, I drank the first peg raw, my throat burned like fire as the drops made their way to my insides burning everything on their way, as it reached my stomach and deposited there, it was like the black flames of Amaterasu, the hell fire. I was overloaded with the memories of her, and I started remembering her, I was feeling light and heavy at the same time. I took two-three shots raw, and I don't remember what happened next, this is I got to know from them the next morning, my head was hurting badly. They said I drank non-stop and started sobbing, crying, attempted to hurt myself, created a ruckus in the hall and terrace. I even said I will jump off from the terrace and even went to attempt but they brought me down, I was shouting in the hall, I was so ashamed on hearing this and I am sorry D, I will not do this again."

"That's something new to take in, how he left all these",-I thought.

"Things had started to normalise, and life has started to heal again, I started to attend classes on a normal basis, my relations with them also healed, I accepted the reality. My relations with Meetu also reached an acceptable level.

D, you remember what the date today was, today was 18th of April, today was Mumma's birthday, we celebrated it nice and she gave a party, she had called in her different friends from different streams and the main highlight was her friend Avani, she was from computer science and engineering department and a close friend of her, Maryam had mentioned her name in the past but I had never met her, but today she looked different, she was wearing plain ethnic and was looking beautiful. Maryam introduced me to her, and she seemed nice, I was at loss of words, and it really made me look dumb in front of her, I wanted to answer but all I can answer was gibberish, God bless Maryam, she came to my rescue and managed the situation well. I was just stealing glances of her, I thought she noticed this. The party went well.

As the responsibility of the National Bachelor's Association, it was the job of every single engineering student to first search for the girl he met on Facebook and then sent her a friend request, so I also did the same; it took an hour for all the research, and I waited for the confirmation, suddenly a notification popped in stating she accepted my friend request. Looks like fortune was on my side, I mustered up all the courage and sent a 'hi' and waited for an answer. Soon I received an answer, and we started to chat. The most obvious question which I asked was 'Do you remember me;

we met today at the party?' She replied back saying she met me today, but she knew me very well as Maryam used to talk about me. The conversation went long and thus numbers were shared and soon we started talking on phone. The duration of the calls increased, and now without knowing we used to talk till late night.

This was the last semester for our seniors, and we had planned a farewell for them. The boys were tasked with outdoor arrangements and the girls with the decorations. Finally, the day arrived, the arrangements completed, and the function started, the guests started to come, it was a beautiful event with performances from Maryam and Shweta, a beautiful medley from our juniors, a band performance from our friends and delicious food.

Our friends from different departments graced us with their presence, and Maryam invited Avani, if words could have described her then it was something like this-When I saw her, this may sound dramatic to u but this is how I felt at that time, my heart skipped a beat or stopped beating altogether for that moment. I was so mesmerized by her elegant charismatic look, it was like an angel has graced me by her presence, and how can anyone be so much beautiful, putting even angels to shame.

Her eyes, my god, were like a maze, once you saw you are bound to lose in it. I can spend my entire life looking in it. They were so pure that sirf ek jhalak mein mohabbat ho jaaye, the eyes were more than enough to bind anyone's soul.

Then comes her hair, free flowing, and wild and when breeze flew her hair, words are not enough to explain anything. The most noticeable feature was her smile, a smile which can even bring life to a deathless soul, agar woh muskura de na toh sab dard taklif bhul jaate the, her smile was so contagious that you are bound to smile with her if she is nearby you. I toh at that time used to steal glances of her and if by any chance she is nearby me, my heart would beat at a higher rate. In short, she was like death has herself arrived to take what is rightfully hers, which was my heart, my soul and in reality, she has succeeded in that.

The event ended with a dance performance, everyone danced their hearts out and I even got a chance to dance with her. Everyone left the place, and I was lost in the events that happened."

"Maybe should I approach her , should I let her know my feelings, do she feel the same, what if she rejects that, these were all the questions I was engulfed with, I couldn't risk my heart breaking once again."

My dear D, I am so frustrated today, today's the worst day t ever exist in my life, Just kidding, a normal day but a blunder happened, thanks to the courtesy of your one and only, Vibhor.

As u know, today was our internal exam scheduled and I didn't even touch the books. So rather than studying for the test, I devised a mastermind plan, which I thought, will be successful. "Par aisi kismat kaha meri", so coming back to plan, I thought of making some cheats and acing the exam and I started working on it, dusting off the dust from the books, opening the chapter and noting down the formulas on the pages very minutely, even the micro xerox would have failed in front of me. And to my surprise, my roommate followed my footsteps.

Dad, you were such a troublemaker! I laughed.

Moreover, today was the weekend and you know what weekend means, the day I will be off to my home, so I packed my stuffs and went to the class, kept my belongings aside and waited for the last period, which was the test time.

The teacher came and handed the question papers to us, and be default, I know nothing. The test duration was of 1 hour, and I just wrote my name and roll number on the answer sheet. Forty minutes has passed and now I took the risk and brought forward my chits, as soon as I opened my chit and tried to scribble it down, much to my dismay, the invigilator caught me and it was no brainer, anyone could have guessed it, someone sitting idly for whole forty minutes and then suddenly started scribbling something on the paper, must have something on him.

Oh, Dad, you must have looked so guilty! I giggled.

Finally, I was caught but that is not the worst part, the worst was yet to come, as you know, in the evening I have to take the train to reach home but when I was caught, the teacher called me up and started lecturing me in front of the whole class, and there time was ticking off, and I was standing there nodding my head.

After an hour of wisdom talks, I was let go.

U know D, I thought I was cleared off all the accusations but my dear I was completely wrong. The invigilator clipped the chit along with the answer sheet and send it off to our HOD, this thing I got to know today at our class end when HOD was distributing our answer sheets. Mine was completely blank with a note clipping to it, and after that there was an enquiry between a criminal who was caught red-handed and the Officer-in-charge.

You poor thing! This just keeps getting better! I cannot control my laughter.

The next few weeks were pure torture. Every faculty member, even lab assistants, took potshots at me whenever they could. So, overall, I was caught cheating, I arrived home late due to the invigilators pravachan and finally I was ragged by the faculties in true sense. That is the story of how I became the laughingstock of the faculty. Cheating? Caught. Late home? Check. Humiliation? You bet.

That was just pure gold, "closing off this chapter shaking my head with amusement and affection."

After that nightmare, I decided never to cheat in internals, rather I will leave the paper blank and prepare for the finals, but dear I won't cheat again. I cleared my bad name by maintaining good decent scores in the finals and gradually increasing them every semester.

Theres multiple stories of our examinations, the one where I failed in one of my papers during my first year, and this was the only time when I have failed in any of my final examinations. As you know, during my first year, I was a frequent home visitor, and my first paper of my semester 1 examination was physics, in which I failed badly as I didn't know the trick, later some of my hostel mates told me that we need to just fill the paper, after that I followed their trick and barely passed the exams.

I cleared that backlog, though some of the teachers help during backlog exams and this time, I was lucky, I copied answers and passed with good marks.

After that incident, I prepared for exams before 10 days in advance and make myself ready for any hurdles.

But during our third-year term, we had a paper of Economics, and our faculty during our classes said with an authority that our department gets easy paper, so we need not to worry, and I followed his words without checking for the previous year papers. Had I checked before, I would have got to know the real scenario. So, on the day of that exam, I was ready with my set of answers, but when question paper was handed out to us, my world turned upside down, I was unable to answer even one single question.

Though I vowed that I will not cheat, that day circumstances forced me to change my vow a little bit and I made my mind to go to the washroom.

What is his obsession with washrooms?

You must be thinking, why washrooms? Students place a copy of organiser or xerox sheets in the washroom, and when they went to the washroom, they sneak-peek into that.

I tried calling mumma, she was sitting ahead of me, she was deep engrossed in writing the answers, after my pleas, she said she will help me after she has completed, but that will take time, so I asked her to just tell me the starting 2-3 lines and rest I will manage. She said ok, but after she has completed half of her exams.

That day, I was sitting idly for one and a half hour, just wrote my name and roll number and the whole page blank. So, I took the risk and went to the washroom, there I saw one of the other department guy, asked him for help, I asked him the 10 marks MCQ and some short questions and the summary of one long question and retuned back to write my paper.

By the time I have remodelled the answers and written, mumma was halfway done, so she helped me with some answers, and I wrote it exactly the same way as Ganesh ji wrote Mahabharat while Ved Vyas ji dictated him the work. After I was done, I was happy that I will pass this, and when results came out, I was happy with the marks.

He is indeed an ancient history geek!

Apart from that, I always completed my exams way before time and even helped my friends with

MCQs and short questions, we had a sign system of telling the answers.

On one exam, I had my completed my answers and waiting for MCQs, so I was sleeping, one of the invigilator poked me and asked me to wake up, as I was disturbing the rest of the class, if I am done, I can submit my paper and leave the class, but I said that some answers are left to fill.

I just went back pretending to write my paper. And when everyone was almost done and 15-20 minutes were left, everyone started using their own morse code to ask for the MCQs. I preferred hand signals, most of the times, and sometimes when teacher is out of the room for a short time, we call out the answers and that helps.

"There is a tradition in our college , a farewell match between the seniors and juniors and an incident occurred, a fight occurred between the players due to a verbal spat which turned into a huge fight , soon the college turned into a battlefield wherein each and every year showing off their strength and supremacy over the other.

Soon it took an ugly turn, and it went out of control, it seemed like any lockdown took place, the seniors threatening the juniors to return to their hostels and not to step outside till everything is over. As evening dawned in the situations worsened, a group of 3rd years decided to teach the 2nd years a lesson, so they marched towards the junior hostels and as news travel faster, the juniors were ready, they lined up on the terrace with glass bottles in their hands, stones chips ready to be fired down. Some guards were placed outside the hostel gate, but on seeing the seniors they also left their guard and ran away along with the warden. The 3rd years took a bamboo stick and were entering the gate, then a glass bottle shattered nearby them, they were to register this but again one shattered near them. They looked up and saw the battalion with their weapons ready to be fired. The juniors shouted if we took one step further then they will hail down the chips and bottles altogether and if anything happens, they are not to be blamed. So, a tactical retreat was taken, and the seniors returned to their base.

Fearing that the situations will get worsened up, the management decided to lock the gates of the 2nd year's hostel gate. It was a wise decision, but as we know confidence when turns to overconfidence, doom is bound to happen. They decided to call up their friends who are residing outside to come and free them from the locks. A group of 40 students entered the campus and straightaway went to break the locks but were unable to do so, so they went a step further, they went to hostel of 3rd year student to teach them their strength.

D, a funny incident happened then, when they were entering the gates, a group of 10 3rd year came out of their hostel to intervene them, seeing those 10 seniors, the group of 40 just disbursed and fled like anything, some fled towards the gate, they were just running here and there. It was just a remarkable sight. Now the 3rd year students were furious, the numbers increased to 50 and went straightaway to the locked down hostels, they broke the locks and entered in purpose of demolishing them. Soon cries were heard as it was a surprise attack, so juniors were not prepared and met their fate. Glass panes were broken, some were slapped hard, and some were beaten with belts and to mark their victory, they burned down a room of the juniors, they stacked mattresses one upon each other and fired it , soon flames engulfed the room and fire brigades were called for the operation.

A day passed by , we all thought that now the situation will be under control, but tables just turned down, a conflict took place between the super seniors which obviously are the 4th year students and the seniors ,that is, the 3rd year ones. We already knew what was to come upon us, so we were prepared already. Our hostel has only one common entry and exit gate, and no other ways to enter in, we locked the channel gates with a big lock from inside, some boys took unused cots to the terrace, and some were busy in grinding the glass bottles into fine powder. We were ready for the battle with our weapons by on our side, soon it took the view of a battlefield with the super seniors marching in with sticks, bottles in their hands, and we the defendants ready for the counterattack, as they were marching in, they were stopped in their tracks by a series of stones chips and then an ultimatum was given to them, if they forward one more step, we will just push the burning cots on them along with the powdered glass will be sprinkled and if anything happens we will not be responsible.

The management got to know of these, they came up with a treaty of ceasefire, but little did they knew that they will be not spared, so one of the faculties got into an argument with the students and got beaten up, now the management got furious, and they complained to the rapid force and asked them to act and thus students were brutally beaten if caught outside. My phone was on silent mode, and I have not viewed it since the start of the fight.

As it cannot go on for long, the defaulters were presented and they apologised and some fines were imposed on them, conditions gradually calmed down, we went to our rooms and sat down to rest, I took out my phone to charge it up, I saw numerous texts and missed calls from my friends, the most interesting was it contained calls and texts from Avani. I called each and every one and explained them everything and asked them not to worry about anything as things had calmed down. Then I called up Avani, she picked up the call and the first thing she asked me where was I? Where had I kept my phone? Why was I not answering? Had anything happened to me, am I safe? She was so tensed, and I can sense her crying, I asked her not to cry and asked her to meet me the next day. She agreed meeting me.

The next day when she met me, the first thing she did was to hit me hard, I actually felt that she was crying now, she was saying she was too tensed and

I didn't care about her, I can't see her cry, I hugged her, I said sorry to her for not informing anything, after a minute or so she stopped crying. I took her to a nearby place and explained her everything. The foolish thing which I did was to propose her straightaway and I thought she would reject me, but she accepted my proposal, I was so happy, and I can see her tears flowing. I hugged her, I wiped off her tears and we sat there for the moment."

OH, proposal amidst the chaos- a perfect name for the situation, "I chuckled."

I and Avani were eagerly waiting for our date. The plan was simple: coffee, a romantic movie, and dinner. I chose my outfit quickly but struggled to find the perfect place. Avani tried various dresses, settling on a stunning black satin dress with a slit and matching heels.

At the cozy coffee shop, we chatted and laughed, sharing stories and dreams. As we strolled through the quiet streets, our hands touched, and Avani entwined her fingers with mine. The evening air filled with tension as we shared a romantic dinner.

As we said goodnight, I leaned in, my eyes locked on Avani's. We shared a tender moment, our hearts beating as one. Avani invited me in, and we sat together, faces inches apart. I held her face close, and we shared a passionate, yet gentle, kiss.

As we sat together, our emotions intensified. We shared intimate moments, our love growing with each passing second. My hands wandered, tracing gentle paths on Avani's skin. We lost ourselves in tender embraces, our love shining brighter.

Our hearts beating as one, they surrendered to deep affection. My lips explored Avani's neck, sending shivers down her spine. We savoured sweet caresses, our love igniting unbridled passion.

My fingers brushed against Avani's soft skin, leaving trails of gentle fire. Avani's soft sighs filled the air as my tender touch ignited deep passion. Our love became all-consuming, every moment precious.

As the night deepened, we lost ourselves in endless kisses and tender whispers. My gentle kisses turned hungry, and Avani's soft moans grew louder. We were lost in all-consuming love, our hearts beating as one.

Time stood still as we cherished every moment. Our love shone brighter with each passing second, filling the night with magical sparks. I and Avani were lost in our own world, where love knew no bounds.

In this world, we found solace in each other's arms. Our love was a safe haven, a place where we could be ourselves. My tender touch ignited deep passion within Avani, and her soft sighs fuelled my desire.

As the night wore on, our love continued to grow. We shared intimate moments, our hearts beating as one. My gentle kisses left Avani breathless, and her soft moans drove me crazy.

Our love was a beautiful dance, a harmonious blend of passion and tenderness. We moved in perfect sync, our hearts beating as one. We were lost in all-consuming love, our every moment precious.

The room was filled with magical sparks, our love illuminating every corner. My eyes locked onto Avani's, and I knew I could not live without her. Avani's heart skipped a beat as my fingers intertwined with hers.

In this moment, time stood still. The world outside melted away, leaving only us. Our love was the only truth that mattered.

As we gazed into each other's eyes, I knew I had to make this moment last forever. I took Avani's hand, leading her to the balcony overlooking the city.

The night sky was ablaze with stars, and the city lights twinkled like diamonds. I turned to Avani, my eyes burning with passion.

"Avani, from the moment I met you, I knew you were special," I said, my voice trembling with emotion. "You light up my world in ways I never thought possible."

Avani's heart swelled with love, her eyes shining with tears.

"Vibhor, I feel the same," Avani whispered, her voice barely audible. "You make me feel alive."

My lips brushed against Avani's, sending shivers down her spine. The world around them melted away, leaving only their love.

In this moment, I knew I had found my soulmate. Avani was my everything, my reason for living.

"I love you, Avani," I declared, my voice filled with conviction.

"I love you too, Vibhor," Avani replied, her voice overflowing with emotion.

As we sealed our love with a kiss, the stars aligned in the sky, witnessing our eternal promise.

In that instant, I and Avani knew our love would last forever.

For my Avani-

'Tum kisi ka khwaab ho
Jo behad khubsurat ho
Iss atrangi duniya mein
Tum bahut pyaari ho

Tere chaand se chehre ko dekhkar
Iss Dil ko thandak mil jaati hai
Unn baadlon se zulfo tale
Thake mann ko rahat mil jaati hai

Teri ankhon ki mithi shararaten
Iss Dil ko bada lubhaayein
Teri pyaari hasi saath mein sabko hasaye
Saath tere na hone ki Kami bahut khal jaaye

Tum naraz hone par badi pyaari lagti ho
Narazgi mein tumhare gaalon pe laali si umad aati hai
Koi gusse mein kaise kamaal lag sakta hai
Ek tum hi toh Jo gusse mein bhi lajawab lagti ho

Tumpar yeh gussa bhi pyaara lagta hai
Gusse mein tumhara muh phulana nyaara lagta hai
Chehre par lalima si nikhar aati hai
Tumpar yeh gussa bhi pyaara lagta hai"

"You are someone's dream, incredibly beautiful
In this strange world, you are very lovely
Looking at your moon-like face
Soothes this heart

Your hair flows like clouds
Gives comfort to this tired mind
The sweet mischief in your eyes
Attracts this heart a lot

Your lovely smile makes everyone smile
Your absence feels like a huge loss
You look even more lovely when you're upset
A pink glow appears on your cheeks when you're angry

How can someone look amazing in anger?
Only you, who looks stunning even in anger
This anger on you also looks lovely
Your pouting face in anger looks cute
A soft glow appears on your face
This anger on you also looks lovely"

Wow, I never knew Dad was into shayaris, he has so beautifully explained his feelings for Ma in this one.

"Our placement seasons were on, and we were tensed about our jobs. I have already fucked up two-three interviews and was sitting for the last core company. Avani has already secured an excellent job in Delhi in an education app company. My interview went well, and I had secured one in Vimta in Hyderabad, and I have to leave in the next week for a month for training purpose. Though the package was less but at least I am not unemployed anymore.

I called up my parents to give them this good news, they were so happy on hearing this news. Days passed on and I went to meet Avani the day before my departure, she came out of her hostel, we met and she asked about my duration, my departure time and every time she asked, I can feel her voice breaking apart, her eyes moistened and she started crying, I was unable to console her and my eyes moistened up too, it was a sight to watch, she found relief in my arms and I found in hers, we just wanted the time to pass like this, we lost the track of time and it was her time to return back to hostel, I was not ready to leave her but it was mandatory.

A month passed by each day felt like a year to us, there was no other way of contacting other than phone calls. On my off day I went to the local market, and I saw an anklet which consisted of pearls in between the chains, it reminded me of her, I bought one for her and kept it safe in my backpack.

I returned after a month, I had missed our farewell party and so the chance of seeing her in that special dress, at first, she was reluctant to attend without me , had to talk to her for a long time just to make her ready to do so. She wore a black saree with red borders to it, her long lanterns like earrings were complimenting her and the medium sized black bindi just completed her look, I wished I was there, Mumma's look was also breathtaking, she too wore a black saree but with a golden plated border with a neck collared blouse to it, she also wore a dangling earring accompanied by a small black bindi. She shared her images to me through WhatsApp.

When I returned back to hostel the first thing I did I went to meet her, she was way so happy on seeing me and so was I, I gave her the anklet she was incredibly happy on receiving them. We spent our day talking about our month and the farewell party.

After 20 days we gave our final exams, and we officially completed our 4 years in HIT. The final day was a memorable one, every 4th year student was spending his or her last moments for the last time with their buddies near our 'four pillars', everyone was drunk, everyone were playing, talking, singing, crying, and were letting their hearts out. It was a remarkable sight. I was resting on Avani's lap with her hands on my hands. Today there was no limitation, no restrictions, no holds barred. The moment was amazing; it was like this misfit has finally got a place to settle in. I just wished the night to be the longest one and I wished to simply just stay there and look into her eyes, she was my moon, my everything for which I can ever hope.

As the night called in, students went to their respective hostels, and mess. I went to leave my princess reluctantly though I never wanted to. As she was leaving, she hugged me and we shared a good kiss, after a moment we broke the kiss and she went to her room, as she reached her room, she opened her window because she knew I wouldn't leave the place unless and until she waves me from her window, she waved me and then I proceeded for my hostel.

I went in my bed but was unable to sleep, I was waiting for the day so that I can actually leave her till the station, and I was planning to go one day late, so maximum of my friends left that day.

I went to pick Avani, she came with her luggage and I met Meetu, Maryam, Shweta and the rest of my friends, so we booked an electric rickshaw and we went to the station, the train reached an hour later, it was a 20 minutes halt at that stop, earlier everyone helped each other board the train and get settled but as soon as the realisations dawned in that this is the very last time everyone will be seeing each other, that hit us hard and suddenly everyone around us started crying, I too started crying on seeing my friends leaving me for the indefinite amount of time, we do make promises to stay in touch, to keep contact but all fails ,that didn't helped my tears falling from my eyes straightaway, I tried not to cry, I tried my hard to hold back my tears but when I saw the faces of my dear ones, it felt like the dam broke, and the same happened to them, they were crying their hearts out, we hugged and cried for a good time, we made promises, we wiped each other's tears and stayed like that for some time ,Avani met her friends and came to bid me goodbye, we knew that it wasn't the last time for us but tears have their own plans , they had decided just to fall off today , I was wiping her face and she was mine, we hugged for the very last time , but time didn't listened to me though this time , the horn of the train honked, everyone boarded the train , before leaving my princess, I kissed her forehead , she too boarded and the train started leaving the platform, everyone was waving either from the windows or from the doors but with still tears in their eyes, I was standing on the platform till the train was very far away from my sight.

I came back to my hostel and packed my stuff and was ready for the next day, some friends of my hostel boarded the train with me, we bid goodbyes to each other and thus four great years ended."

Well it's been months since we graduated and we were working at our respective locations, I have been to Delhi once in a while, we were enjoying our company but something was bothering her, she didn't mentioned anything but I was sensing it, the way she used to chirp earlier now has almost became silent, I tried asking her several times D , but she always just buzzed it off saying it to be the work pressure.

I have been thinking something from the past few months, it's the high time that I should propose her D and I will do it by the next week, as it will be her birthday and I can't wait anymore. I have planned everything; I will be spending my entire day with her and at dinner I will ask her out to be my everything for the rest of my life.

Later after that day…………

D, I hate my life , I asked for one thing and that one thing only mattered to me, wait D I will explain everything to you, the day started well, we went for a movie and after that went for a shopping spree, I was getting the one thing which I was missing out , her smile, we went for a walk and then to a nearby restaurant , I ordered for a cake and for surprise when she cut the cake I proposed her, but she asked me to stop and said she can't answer and just walked out of the restaurant.

I cannot believe she did not accept the proposal, was she goofing around me all this time? I know it is too soon, but we can plan our future together, I see my future with her only. You know I tried calling her many times, I even dropped texts, but she is not replying to any of my texts. What should I do now?

It has been weeks she is avoiding me, I returned back to Hyderabad but cannot get myself out from that day, I have decided to confront her for the last time, I am going this weekend and will get myself a closure.

When my flight landed, I straightaway went to her place, in that way she can't ignore me, I reached her place and then rang up the bell, she came to open the door and was shocked on seeing me, I let myself in and then eventually we started talking in a bit civilised manner initially and then the civilisation just gone extinct like it never existed. I was adamant on getting my answers and she was reluctant to answer anything. I asked for the final time that is that she wants that I am out of her life and to my surprise with tears in her eyes she said yes.

There is this only one thing which I can't bear and that is, tears in her eyes, seeing her crying I cannot control my tears and asked is this she really wants, the answer took me aback, she said she cannot ruin my life and she wants to see me happy, I was confused, how come she was ruining my life but she will completely ruin my life if she is not a part of my life, I reasoned with her, I straightaway cleared her that if she is not a part of my life, I don't want my life.

Eventually she gave in and told me the truth that she is suffering from a critical illness which will eventually take her life in a few years; she questioned me whether I will take anyone whose life is unsure, I quietly left the place and went outside, she thought it was obvious of anyone to leave when heard of any situation. I came back inside and took her to a place, she was confused as of where I am taking her, we drove for a few minutes and reached our destination and the destination was the office of the court magistrate, she was all confused and I told my answer to her question that even if it is for a while I won't step back out, I want my forever with you only, she had tears in her eyes, and we went inside with the proceedings and we were officially married.

We broke the news of our marriage to our parents and they were really happy, we asked them to come to Delhi for the rituals and here I asked my company to give me a posting in here Delhi only, the formalities were done within a week, we were happy, we were having a gala time, this was the one and only thing which I wanted, her smile.

One day we were casually talking, and she expressed her desire for a child, and I couldn't agree less with her, I too wanted a child as beautiful as her, the exact replica of her and we came to a common conclusion that we should adopt one child, the news really made her happy and seeing her happy I was happy too. We started searching for adoption agencies and orphanages and one day we went to one after filling all our details. We reached there and went to their office and after filling all the details, we went inside the room. And you will not believe me D, the very moment we saw teetu, we knew she was the only one , we made our mind on adopting her , we expressed our desire on adopting teetu and by God's grace we got all the necessary permissions, and we were officially parents.

"Ohh this is how I was inducted to this family; I felt a tear just fall out on knowing all these."

Today, I and Avani celebrated our first anniversary, a year filled with laughter, tears, and unforgettable moments. We planned surprises to make this day extraordinary.

I carefully selected a stunning ring and pendant, symbols of our eternal love. I brought a bouquet of Avani's favourite flowers and a bottle of fine wine. Avani, meanwhile, transformed our home into a romantic haven, adorning it with scented candles and dim lights. She cooked my favourite dinner, filling the air with savoury aromas.

As I returned home, Avani lit the candles, bathing our space in warm, golden light. The fragrance of roses and lavender enveloped me, and I felt my heart skip a beat.

"Avani, you've outdone yourself," I whispered, my eyes locked on hers.

Avani smiled, her eyes sparkling. "I wanted tonight to be special."

Our candlelight dinner was a sensory delight. We savoured each bite, sharing stories and laughter. I presented Avani with the ring and pendant, and her eyes welled up with tears.

"Avani, from the moment I met you, I knew you were the one," I said, my voice trembling.

Avani's heart swelled with emotion. "Vibhor, I love you more with each passing day."

As we finished dinner, Avani revealed her surprise. She disappeared into the bedroom, emerging in a breathtaking red gown.

My jaw dropped. "Avani, you're stunning."

Our lips met in a passionate kiss, the world around us melting away.

As the night deepened, I and Avani shared a romantic and sensual dance, our bodies swaying to the rhythm of love. The dim lights and soft music created an intimate ambiance, and we felt like we were the only ones in the world.

My hands traced gentle paths on Avani's skin, sending shivers down her spine. Avani's eyes locked onto mine, and she felt her heart flutter. We moved in perfect sync, our bodies entwined.

Our dance was a beautiful expression of our love, a sensual and emotional connection that left us both breathless. My fingers brushed against Avani's skin, leaving trails of gentle fire.

My hands roamed Avani's body, exploring every curve and contour. Our lips met in soft, gentle kisses, and they felt like they were melting into each other.

As we cuddled, feeling each other's warmth, I knew this anniversary was unforgettable.

"I love you, Avani," I whispered.

"I love you too, Vibhor," Avani replied.

Our hearts beat as one, filled with magical sparks.

As we drifted off to sleep, my arms wrapped around Avani, holding her close.

"Forever and always," I whispered.

"Forever and always," Avani echoed.

I shouldn’t be reading the details of their intimate moments, but it’s so beautifully penned down, they were indeed a perfect match.

The rest of the pages are blank, where's the rest of the story. There are some torn pages folded inside, it has some stained marks on it.

You know D, this past few weeks were harsh on me , life has been unfair to me and my God has been snatched away from me.

We lost Papa on an unfateful night. I cannot describe what we were going through these past few days. One day suddenly we have to become adults , taking decisions on our own, and living by them.

Prior to that day, I was just a stupid adult stepped into adulthood, earning money for myself, enjoying life to my fullest, but now we are suddenly the bread earners of the family. I do not want any of this, I just want to be the stupid brat who knows that his father is with him, his father will take care of everything, he need not to be worried about anything, he can still live his life on his own terms.

I never thought I will see this day in my life, my hands are still shaking while thinking about that night, how we carried him to the hospital wherein hordes of doctors ganged on to check for vitals, how I was just standing outside helplessly seeing my life fade into oblivion.

My heart stopped beating at that time when the doctors called me inside and they let me know that my universe is crumbled, and my father is not with us anymore. When I heard, I lost my sense of understanding, I felt like the ground was pulled from under me, still there was the hardest thing to do at that point of time, letting my brother and mother know.

When I came outside of the room, I was unable to speak anything and when bhai asked me about what doctor said, I was just able to nod my head, it felt like my words left my mouth, I can't speak anything, at that point we all three broke into tears and we were unable to console each other. It was the longest day of my life which ended by taking away my strength, my happiness, my support system.

The worst was yet to come, we reached our native place for final rites and cremation. At that point, my heart broke into thousand pieces, I did not want to live, how can anyone live seeing the man who nurtured your life , seeing him burn in front my eyes, the hands which caressed my cheeks was burning in front my eyes to ash. Fire engulfed him and I was there standing, unable to do anything.

After the rites were over and some days passed by, I gathered the broken pieces of my heart and some courage and returned to our home. With the passing days, life went to normalcy for others, but it will take some time for us, it feels like a void is still there, just finding some reasons to fill the gap, He is still among us, gracing us with his aura, even if I take several lifetimes, still I can't be the man He was.

You know D, papa was very fond of kids, sometimes, I think My kid will not get the love, if he were still here and I had a baby, he would have ushered everything on his grandchild. The kid would have been the luckiest fellow here.

Life's unfair sometimes and with some people, and we are that some people.

The very next morning. Out of curiosity at the breakfast table, I asked Dad. Tell me something about dadu. How was he?

Papa asked, how come you are asking about this out of nowhere? I said I just felt like asking you.

Papa patted my head and started saying with a gleam in his eyes, " he was the most patient dad one could ever ask for; he was the one even he had nothing in his pocket, he would never ever decline his kids demands any day and he was the best-looking dad and the most important thing, the best chef in the world".

"And moreover," he added, "if he were alive, you would have been the luckiest kid around, he would have pampered you the most. I still miss him," he said while reminiscing his good old times.

I am writing this with tears stained on my cheeks and a heavy heart. In the hollow of her departure, I search for words to pen it down for the last time. My whole life is in pieces and has been shattered to the very core, and I do not think I will be able to write anything again.

Have you seen in the beaches, we build the sandcastles, and those sandcastles gets washed away by the waves, even if we try to hold that together by any means , it ends up crumbling down, the same way, my life has been turned upside down, the foundation of my world had crumbled.

This was the second instance which fucked up my happy life, first the death of my father which shook the foundation, but she and my other family members stabilised me and now the death of my supporting pillar which shattered the foundation.

She has left me, left me alone to stay miserable in this fucking world. She was my world; she meant everything to me.

"Ma was your world, but you're mine now, Daddy."

She was the words to my writing, the music to my songs, the essence of my life. She was the smile on my face.

She was indeed a fighter, a warrior who battled till her last breath, she was in a lot of pain, but she endures that she kept a smile on her face just for the sake of me.

Mommy was brave. I want to be brave like her.

She knew if I saw her crying I would have broken down and that she did not want. I remember her smile, weak but defiant, as she whispered, "I'll beat this." Her determination inspired me, even in the darkest moments. Her strength was contagious, and I drew from it every day.

Daddy, you are brave too. You took care of Ma and me

We both knew this was bound to happen, but it happened way too soon. She was happy, and I was happy too, seeing her smile every day despite all odds, enjoying the company of her little princess, ushering her with all love she had.

The days we had together were a gift. I cherish the memories of our lazy Sundays, our spontaneous adventures, and our quiet nights spent talking about dreams and fears. Her love was my anchor, my safe haven.

"Your love is my anchor too, Daddy."

Now, I will honour her legacy, striving to filling the void in our daughter's life with the love and devotion she wanted to give, I will hold onto these memories, keeping her spirit alive.

"You are doing your part exactly the same way you promised to Ma, and I am sorry for the days when I misunderstood you, I am extremely sorry," a tear rolled down the cheek.

"What is this? A letter hidden inside the diary, let me open and see what is in it," it is a letter written by mom for dad.

"It pains me a lot while writing this letter , if the situation was different I wouldn't have written one, I am so lucky to have you in my life, I wouldn't have thought that you will be an important person in my life, we made innumerable memories together but you complete me, you are the reason for my happiness every moment now and then, but it hurts me when I think I won't be able to spend the rest of my life with you, the moments we met, our first date, our relationship, your proposal, our marriage, our child , are the things you gave me.

After I am gone, please take loving care of our teetu, do not let her feel out, she is our last memory together, do see that she is always happy, she is our princess. She is such a gentle soul, please look after her, she already had a hard time before, don't let my absence affect her.

No one has ever made me feel special the way you made me Vibhor, you gave me everything but never asked for anything in return, when I am gone do not cry for me, I will be with you always in your heart, I will be with you always in the form of our little princess, I want our each and every moment to be special.

You made me complete; I cannot thank you enough for what you have done for me, my life was in a mess, and you fixed it, you made me feel special, you made me feel alive.

Can you do one last favour; just let teetu know that her mother is very much sorry to leave her like these, just let her know that her mother loved her to the very last moment of her life, she is proud to be her mother and will be proud always, she will always look after her.

Your loved partner,
Avani"

"This diary is full of surprises for me and will be my precious treasure for me till the last breath".

The Last Note

"Another note in the diary; this is from dad, let's see what he has for me."

"*Sorry teetu, sorry for not being able to take care of you, sorry for not being there to watch you grow into a beautiful princess. Sorry for everything I promised but failed to fulfil.*

Do not be angry with me for a longer period of time, I won't be able to bear that, I didn't want to leave you like this but had to, I personally had no say in that, but don't think I have left your side, I will be always with you, in your heart, seeing my love becoming an inspiration for everyone.

You know teetu you were the best thing that has ever happened to me, you were the brightness to my dark world, when I first saw your smiling face, the void in my life was filled up, I was empty, but you completed me, this misfit finally found a place to rest, finally found a place which I can call home.

I have seen time changing so fast wherein young lives lost so quickly that they did not have any chance to display their love, their views to anyone. I am also not different, time won't stop for me Or give me another chance, I hadn't drunk the nectar of immortality that I will be alive for centuries, if I am getting one chance to leave something from my experiences for the present and future, I won't hesitate to do so.

My experiences are not the experiences of mine but the experiences of people I met, the people I read about, the people who taught me, the people I conveyed.
Time changes so fast and people changes even faster than that, I am not making any verdict that I won't change in the coming future but the thing which do not changes are our principles, our ethics, our efforts.

Maybe I won't be there to witness the change, but I want to make a mark in this world. I am not the ideal one, not the ideal son, an ideal friend, an ideal student, and even an ideal human being, I am full of flaws.

A day will come when I will be lying lifeless, my family and friends will mourn for a while and then the world will heal for them, but the thing which will remain forever are my deeds, my work, my art, my principles.

My word for the future is that if you made any mistake don't fear rather learn from it, you are going to have lot of flaws , accept it with a smile, never compromise your principles but remember to make good decision between good and bad, never bully others on the basis of looks, their work.

No work is small, treat every work with great respect , respect those who deserves it, never judge anyone without knowing the 3 sides of the story, there's no shortcut to hard work, you have a fire inside of yourself, never let it diminish, be compassionate to others, learning has no age and try to learn from everyone without discrimination.

Learn from my mistakes, my experiences but don't be like me, I am not asking you be the ideal kid but be the one you want, you will have your own freedom of life, be whatever you want to become, maybe I won't be with you forever and maybe I won't be able to see you grow up, but remember my words will be with you and I will be proud of you always.

I never left your side, even though my life has stopped but I will continue to live in you, I know you can do it; you are a part of me. The last note will be with you always."

"Some last words in form of my shayari for my Teetu".

"O meri ladaku ,sunn Rahi ho kya
Abhi toh Gaye kuch pal hi beetein
Khafa mujhse yu hogayi kya

Chahta tha kuch der aur thahar jaun
Waqt tere saath kuch pal aur bita jaun
Par shayad yeh meri takdeer nahi
Shayad badi meri umr nahi

Tere saath chalne ka wada tha
Tere pankho ko udaan Dene ka irada tha
Lamha kuch aur agar shayad tujhe de paata
Mann ka ho jaata toh kya hi baat thi

Pata hai tu thodi khafa hogi
Ruth kar shayad kuch pal baat bhi na karegi
Par zindagi ka alam kuch yu hai

Meri bhi toh kuch majburi thi samjha kar

Tere kadmo ko badhta dekhna chahta tha
Tujhe safalta ki unchaiyon par dekhne ka irada tha
Tere har Khushi mein Tere saath rehna chahta tha
Tujhe yu majhdhar mein akela nahi chorna chahta tha

Tu royegi toh dard se tadap jaunga
Tere anshu ponchne ko main yu taras jaunga
Marr ke bhi chain nahi paunga
Tu hi bata aise kaise main mukti paunga

Ek aakhri dafa bas tujhe dobara gale lagana hai
Tere mathe ko bas pyaar se ekbaar chumna hai
Bas yahi kehna hai ki mujhe tujhpe naaz hai
O meri ladaku,kya tumne Kiya mujhko maaf hai"

"Oh my beloved, are you listening?
Only a few moments have passed, and you're already upset with me.
Why are you angry? I wanted to spend more time with you.
I wanted to cherish every moment with you.

But perhaps it's not my destiny.
Perhaps my life isn't long enough.
I promised to walk with you,
To give your wings the freedom to fly.

If only I could give you a few more moments.
If only it were possible, what wonder it would be!

I know you're upset, and perhaps you won't speak to me.

But life is cruel, and I have my compulsions too.

I wanted to see you grow and succeed.
I wanted to see you reach new heights.
I wanted to share every joy with you.
I didn't want to leave you alone in difficult times.

If you cry, I'll be tormented by pain.
I'll yearn to wipe away your tears.
Even death won't bring me peace.
You're the only one who can free me.

Just one last time, I want to hold you close.
Just once more, I want to gently kiss your forehead.
I just want to say that I'm proud of you.
Oh my beloved, have you forgiven me?"

“They just made me emotional; I love them very much. I will keep this diary with me always, and this handwritten letters from both Ma and Dad are my treasures, I won’t lose them”.

ABOUT THE AUTHOR

Bikky Rai, debut author and engineer by profession, is a writer by passion. Born and raised in Santragachi, West Bengal, India, Bikky draws inspiration from life experiences and imagination. Join Bikky's literary journey on Instagram **@misfit_vaani**.

www.ingramcontent.com/pod-product-compliance
Lightning Source LLC
LaVergne TN
LVHW091223150826
845673LV00003B/987

* 9 7 9 8 8 9 6 1 0 0 8 5 0 *